Waitii

The girl with the ball is waiting behind...

the man with the towel, who is waiting behind...

the woman
with the hat,
who is waiting
behind...

the boy with the skateboard,
who is waiting behind...

the woman with the bag,

who is waiting behind...

my dog and me.

Do you know what we are all waiting for?

Ice cream.